THE POETIC ART
OF SEDUCTION

By

Clarissa O. Clemens

Table of Contents

I would like to dedicate this book to all the beings that have stimulated my mind and body – you ignited a torch that cannot be extinguished and will always burn deep.

I would like to express my love and appreciation for all my friends and family who encouraged me toward my goals. A special thanks to the Young Buck, the Angel, Wendela, and my wonderful Man – my first audience.

To my Man, life partner, lover, and best friend – I love you, Tom B. forever and all ways.

Ode to O

Reeling
Feeling
Biped kneeling
Squealing
Screaming
Bouncing off the ceiling
Deep and tight
Don't say goodnight
Splendid flow
Spectacular O

Levels of Ecstasy

Levels of ecstasy fogging my brain
Shooting off pleasure peaks
Cusping near pain
Nails digging deep into flesh soft and white
Tingling sensations triggers me tight

Release the tension growing inside
Setting the stage feeling you glide
Shuttering waves ruffling through my heart
Slipping within our bodies won't part

No space in between
True mergence foreseen
The passion plunging emotional twirls
Giving our toes a permanent curl
Gripping & grasping with all my might
Yielding desires incredible sight

Lifting to meet you completely open
Breathing so fast racing heartbeats hoping
Skin moistened salty and sweet
Our nectars combining radiating heat
Ultimate conquest saturated slumber
In your arms I don't need to wonder

Gasp Grasp Glee

Fill up my grip
Don't let it slip
Out of my grasp
Letting out a gasp
Of delight and glee
Don't get away from me
The plan I have in store
Is to give you more and more
Of pleasure true and strong
With every move
You can't go wrong

Urges Unchained

Feeling the surges of urges unchained
Thinking the thoughts a little bit deranged

Warm waves of wetness wash over my soul
Wanting to surrender and lose control

Allowing the thoughts to take over me
To send me reeling in ecstasy

Taking you with me on a wild ride
Anticipating the sensation of you growing inside

Pushing out my desires to the lining of my being
Reaching out to you positioned and kneeling

Parted and melted you spread me around
Aiming erect in our nectars we drown

Honey-coated humans a delectable treat
The taste of your essence ultimately sweet

To bathe in the glow of true lovers bliss
To seal our union with a captivating kiss

Bent to be Taken

Bent to be taken
Broken and shaken
Full spread probe
Nibble bitten lobe
Stroke to provoke
Smack and attack
Flaccid knees
Hard on squeeze
Swollen flowin
Moaning growing
Lifted limbs
Squirm and swim
Gush and glow to and fro

Bound to be taken
Secured for the spankin
Halfway to pain
Pleasurable gain
Sweet smell of lust
Impeccable trust
Given to desire
Flames of fire
Dance between screams
Nightmares and dreams
Overcome
Come all over

Clarissa O. Clemens

Devour with Power

Dripping glistening hard and thick
Salivating anticipating grab and lick
Stroke and poke eager lips
Devour with power legs and hips

Straddle the saddle ready for the ride
Whip and wrangle your succulent hide
Grab the reins I'm in control
Steer and guide you toward my honey dripping flow

Search and slide probe and glide
With a nibble and bite tight delight
Drops of sweat mingle and tingle
Sensitized skin lingering finger

Touch and taste tantalizing mixture
Sweet yet bitter warm breathe of a whisper
Tickling your ears stimulating your soul
Complete we merge to fill the hole

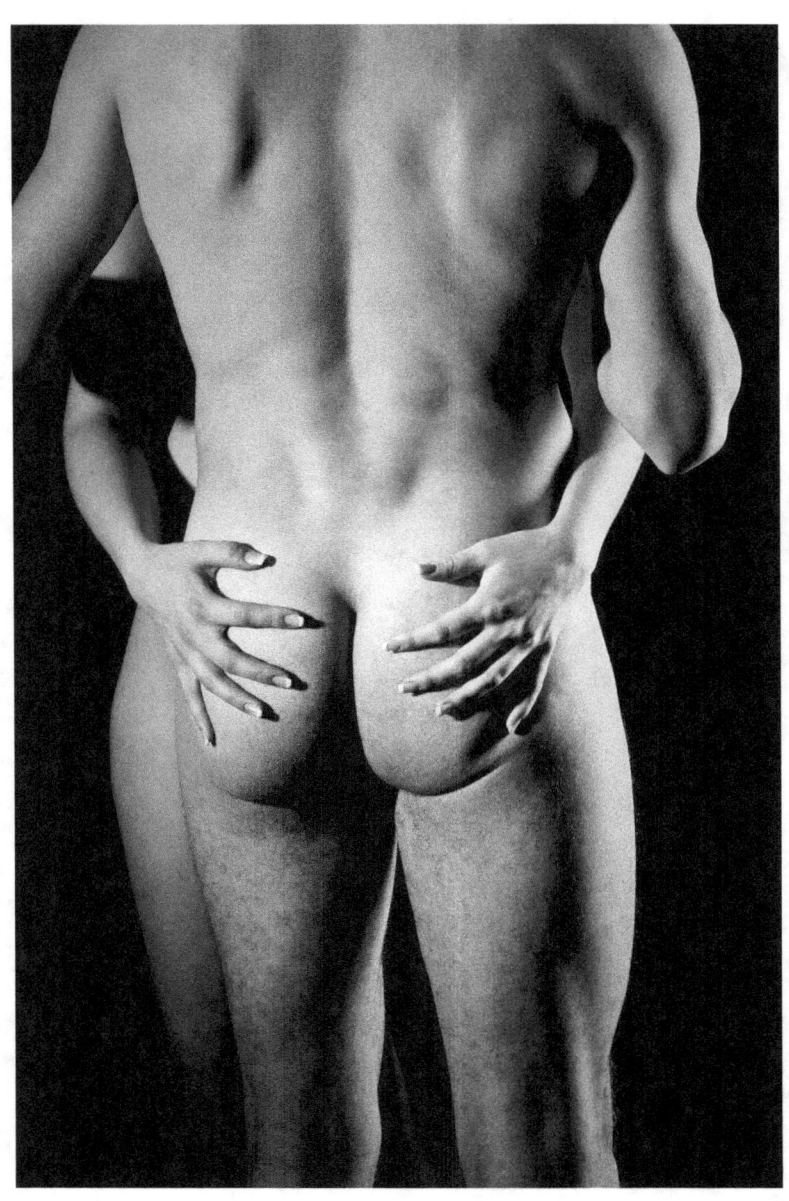

Shapes of desire

Cumulus clouds capture my crime
Shapes of desire frozen in time
Erotic images saturate my mind
Soaked in sensuality reality behind

The taste the texture luring me in
Drawing me closer to touch naked skin
A fingers' length away, just beyond reach
Dripping wet, sweet succulent peach

Take a bite the dream is real
Slip through the vapors, a warm form I feel
Floating on fantasy
With head in the clouds
Dream taking shape
Solid to steal
Drifting back to the now in time
Determined to make real
Everything in my mind

Known intent

Man of mysterious outcome
Come out and play with me
Man with magnetic ways
Please have your way with me

The contrast of your masculinity
Accentuates my femininity
Striking the match of passion
Blazing rising flames of desire

Woman with known intent
Intending to explore
Woman with her senses on the edge
Edging for some more

The interplay of fantasy
Plays off our ecstasy
Entering your treasure chest
Devour your jewels a licking fest

United excited merging our flesh
In the lap of seduction
Our union feels fresh

Teardrop of Pleasure

They all have a load
Waiting to explode
With the pull of his trigger
Watching it grow bigger
Taking the tip
slowly to my lips
Teardrop of pleasure
Becomes my treasure
Whispering into his ear
So he can hear me clear
I will send him to a place
With no time or space
Handling him with care
Directing his body with flair
Urgent need to succeed
In his plead
To stroke and hold
And allow the unload
Finding the spot
My tongue has been taught
To flick and lick
Rigid and thick
Seeing him shudder
My name is uttered
Begging please to take him
With a tight squeeze
Forcing the eruption
Dominated by seduction
Relieved to succeed
Completing the deed

Squirming

Squirming in my seat
Anticipating the heat
Growing in your lap
A fluid fountain to tap
Pair of lips
Parallel hips
Positioned square
Slippery dare
Climb up fantasies
Searching for ecstasy
Inch by inch
With a flick and a flinch
Encrypted coding
Cues to unloading
When you start your moaning
With the pleasure I'm loaning
To receive
To relieve
To tease
and please…

Take Me

Urgent
Subservient
Take me
Shake me
Quake deep
A melted heap
Dripping wet
Drops of sweat
Throbbing pulsation
Deep felt sensation
Hard and fast
Made to last
Flood of passion
Pure satisfaction

Anticipation

Anticipation high
For sweet pleasures
In the night
Long break alone
Absence of moans
Leading to longing
Yearning dethonging
Throbbing and flogging

Pleasure portal posed
Passion exposed
Spread sublime
Succulent and primed
Deep and tight
Memories invite
Visions entwined
Losing my mind

Capture my heart
Please let us start
Waiting for a touch
Tender and lush
Electric my skin
Tingling within
Surrender to bliss
Breathless kiss

Wanton Wiles

Are you really that wild?
Let me get you riled
Shoot shudders up your spine
Tantalize tickle and dine
On wanton wiles worked up
Filling up my cup
Running over to kiss your lips
Planting nirvana my tongue slips
Inside your mind wandering
Hands roam while pondering
How close can we get?
Steamy wet dripping sweat
Converge submerge
Covered in you

Luscious Hands of Fate

Parting with a potent sigh
Release control muscular thigh
Apart and smooth silky touch
Taking our time never rush
Explore your door to pleasure
Finding your hidden treasure
Massaging the thoughts that stimulate
Guided by luscious hands of fate
Feeling warmth gliding along
Listening dreamily to our favorite song
A beautiful connected loving dance
Bodies in rhythm almost in trance
A different level of knowing
Complete in sync and flowing
Skin electric sensitivity heightened
Explosive release spirit enlightened
Surrender soul to feel whole
Close to God close to you
Close to me feelings true

Stroke it

Stroke it
Choke it
I can provoke it

Tease it
Squeeze it
Please release it

Spew
On cue
The only thing to do

Receive
Relieve
Never grieve

I want
The taunt
Complete we meet

Ooze then snooze
You're the one
I choose

Cuddled tight
Sweet delight
Turn off the light
Goodnight

Feather Cream

Eagle feather standing straight
Creamy colored erotic fate
Tickling tendrils teasing twist
Sweat so salty steamy mist
Rising pleasure climbs the vine
Blood flow surging feeling fine
Erupting waves shoot up your spine
At one with self supreme sublime

Feminine Skin

Your feminine skin
Makes me want to reach within
The softness invites
Sensuous nibbles and bites

As your breath exhales
I strive for your moans and wails
The part of you I find
So deep so tight so divine

Is yearning for my touch
Looking into your eyes as you blush
My fingers tease and tantalize
Traveling softly slowly up your thighs

Quivering ripples collide between us
Charging electric surges of lust
Finding my way drawn by your heat
In search of your nectar so sticky and sweet

Your body arches as it yearns and burns
My mouth explores you as I watch you churn
The anticipation builds as I find your spot
Tip of tongue flickering hot

Sparks of desire ignite your fire
Shuttering waves taking you higher
To that plain of pleasure
Watching you in beauty and splendor

Pulling you open I pulse and probe
As my excitement builds I completely disrobe
Feeling you grab me the intensity builds
Tensing your muscles with me you're filled

Spreading you open soaking up the view
The final plunge sends me deep inside of you
Rising and falling exhilaration takes over
Our bodies entwined ultimate lover
Massive magnitude melds our mounds of flesh
Shockwaves shaking pleasured fresh

Nuance

Finding every nuance
To please you
To touch,
Just so
secret spot
Wave of a sweeping kiss
Caress and mesmerize
Lips that hypnotize
Take you to
The moan zone
Erotically flown
Over your landing pad
The best I ever had
Sweetly swell
Dangling drop
Body slowly melts
The urge for you
Never stops

Reunion

Dance me sensual
Artistically poetic
Touch consensual
Intuitively empathic
Free flow caress
Slipping down my dress
Skin drenched sweat
Intertwined and wet
Passionate urges
Erotic surges
Years in between
I like what I'm seeing
Would love another dance
A chance of romance

Clarissa O. Clemens

Touch to Taste

Languorous limbs
Laying limp
Tangled together
Succulent silky skimp
Erotic electric sensation
Slippery smooth move
Within my skin
Upon my chin
Your lips caress
The kiss suggests
The love within
Embraced and pure
Connected secure
Touch to taste
Not a drop to waste
Each precious drop
I don't ever want to stop
The flow of you
Combining the two
You with me
Through eternity

Melt me

Melt me and
Spread me around
Lapping the sweetness
Ecstasy found
Open inviting
Body surprising
Arching tease
Wide wonder
Wicked wiles
Lightening and thunder
Destiny trials
Dripping off the edges
Peering over ledges
Dip for a taste
Exquisitely embraced

Licking the corner

Succulent pursed
Lips parted
Heaving breath
Chest pounding
Fingertips reach
Your electric
Skin softened
Creamy folds
Of silky
Sensuous desires
Open to me
Sinking in
Engulfed and enveloped
Into your need
Licking the corner
Of your life

A Melted Heap

The beat in the heat of the night
No fight or fright
Ready for flight

Sinking deep a melted heap
Sweet taste dripping
Off my tongue
Plunge
Into your life

Absorbing the essence
That makes up you
Tantalizing breath
Whisper in my ear

Opportunity exists unknown
Open fists resist
The oneness alone
Pushing forward
Engulf me
Please persist

Clarissa O. Clemens

Glistening

Glistening
dew drizzled day
Languid limbs
lazily longing
Arched
in anticipational array
Sprawled
deliciously hanging

Warm breath
sneaks a caress
Behind my ear
and down my back
touch teasing
start to undress
Flip me over
sensuous attack

Surrender panting
pliant await
Your next move deliberate
Sustain heightened state

Wrists wrestle wrangle
Lips Tingle tangle
Strength succumb submission
Parting pensive passion

Melted mounds
moaning merging
Sensual sounds
slowly surging

Peaked
sweat streaked skin
Slippery heat
soaked from within
Turgid
pink puffed prize
Linger between
spread open thighs

Nudge an inch
Gripping to pinch
Fit to be tied
Tightest of fits

Quiver and quake
Simmering snake
Boiling and flowing
Oozing and glowing

Pinned down and probing
Pleasure evoking
Words in my ear
Warm flush and a tear

Take my gift
Feel my heart shift
Keep it from breaking
Body and mind aching

For You

Tongue Tied

Sweet succulent parting lips
Opening petals welcoming bliss
Flowering honey drops moistened tips
Tongue takes a taste lasting kiss

Dancing energy surges within
Sparks fly flicker and spin
Eyes covered, restrained limbs
Spread and waiting I feel your sin

A touch comes from somewhere
A grab of my hair
Hot breath arouses and shoots off flares
Vulnerably open I can sense your stare

Electricity charging through my veins
Tingling and toying driving me insane
Intense waves of pleasure bordering on pain
Riding on peaks, rising on flames

Vibrating buzz travels up my thighs
A kiss on my neck release of a sigh
Hands pinned down, legs opened wide
As the tip enters I let out a cry

Probing and pulsing penetrate please
Parted and fluttering entering with ease
Teeth at my neck, breeze at my knees
Tormenting with pleasure erotic tease

Surrender to strength acquiesce release
Full penetration passion peaks
Body saturated feeling weak
Untied unleashed unable to speak

Release & Quiver

Opening my body,
For you to devour
The subtleties of pleasure,
Are in your power
Mounting maneuver,
Release and quiver
A touch deep inside,
Triggers a shiver
Losing control,
I shudder and shimmer
Vibrating thighs, heavy sighs
Let go a glimmer
Building and climbing
Tightened and ready
Clenching and gripping
Rocking so steady
Unraveling avalanche
Rips though my core
Grabbing the rush
Riding towards more
Over and over this feeling of bliss
Culminates and crumbles under your kiss

Teetering heart

Do you feel the warm
Dripping nectar unleashed
Full moistness of lips
Parted and panting
Ecstasy around the edge
Teetering heart beating
Rush the quivering
Thighs to resist
Revealing my desire
Glistening gap unfold
Invite you to enter
Release fluttering feeling
Nirvana achieved

Sizzle

Sizzle of your swizzle stick
Can I take a luscious lick?
Melt your marshmallow in search of crème
Place my lips upon your dream

Take the heat inside my mouth
Traveling tongue heading south
Strawberry-shaped succulent slip
Riding the ridge gentle flip

Encircle circumference hard and thick
Encompass your muscle
Slide in quick
Sweet dewy drop invites a taste
Slippery and warm in a honey-baste

When your eruption rises and flows
The magnitude shakes you from your head to your toes
I welcome the warm surges of your delectable nectar
Swallowing your essence an intoxicating mixture
Sending me on an erotic high
Joining you as we float and fly
To that place of peak perfection